Mole in Goal

by **Amanda Brandon**
illustrated by **Giusi Capizzi**

Mole loved football.

He wanted to be in a team.

But he couldn't see very well and his little feet were not good at kicking.

He bounced his ball too high.

The ball splashed in the pond.

Then it shot into the vegetable patch.

Rudy Rabbit dodged out of the way.

Mole tried again.

This time he smashed the ball into

Badger's greenhouse!

"Grr!" Badger took the football away.

One day, Mole spotted the River Rats playing in the park.

"Can I play with you?" Mole said.

The rats laughed.

"A mole kick a ball? That's impossible!"

Rudy Rabbit was digging up carrots.

"I'll never play for a team," Mole said.

"I can't see the ball and my feet

are too small."

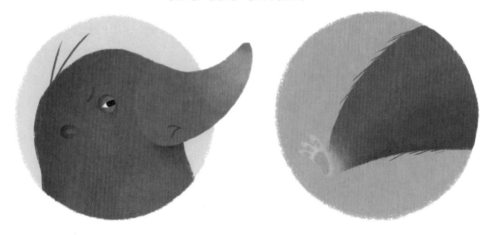

He helped Rudy pull out carrots. His big
front paws pulled five bunches at a time.

Rudy said, "You could be a goalkeeper with those big paws. You can play on our team."

Mole was pleased. "But how will I see the ball?" he asked.

Rudy made a special rattling ball

so Mole could hear it.

Mole practised listening for the ball.

He got better and better.

Soon it was the day of the big match:

River Rats V Rabbit Rovers.

Mole saw something zoom towards him.

He thought it was the ball. He dived but...

"Caw caw!" It was a crow.

"Oops, sorry!" Mole said.

The River Rats laughed and their

striker scored.

"Don't listen to them," Rudy said.

"Listen for the ball."

With one minute left, the score was

2-1 to Rabbit Rovers.

River Rats took a penalty.

Mole heard the ball.

Whoosh!

It was on Mole's right.

He stretched out his big paws and dived...

Mole saved the ball just as

the final whistle blew!

Everyone cheered for Mole.

"Well done, Mole," Rudy said. "We make a great team. And our team will always need..."

"...a mole in goal!"

Quiz

1. What sport does Mole love to play?
a) Tennis
b) Football
c) Netball

2. Why does Mole think he can never join a team?
a) He can't see the ball very well
b) There are no teams to join
c) His back paws are too big

3. What does Rudy use to help Mole?
a) A special ball that rattles
b) Magic gloves
c) Glasses

4. Who are the Rabbit Rovers playing at the big match?

a) Crazy Cats

b) River Rats

c) Dotty Dogs

5. What does Mole think is the ball during the match?

a) A carrot

b) The sun

c) A crow

Turn over for answers

Book Bands for Guided Reading

The Institute of Education book banding system is a scale of colours that reflects the various levels of reading difficulty. The bands are assigned by taking into account the content, the language style, the layout and phonics. Word, phrase and sentence level work is also taken into consideration.

Maverick Early Readers are a bright, attractive range of books covering the pink to white bands. All of these books have been book banded for guided reading to the industry standard and edited by a leading educational consultant.

To view the whole Maverick Readers scheme, visit our website at

www.maverickearlyreaders.com

Or scan the QR code above to view our scheme instantly!

Quiz Answers: 1b, 2a, 3a, 4b, 5c